First published in Great Britain by HarperCollins Children's Books in 2004
HarperCollins Children's Books is a division of HarperCollins Publishers Ltd.

1 3 5 7 9 10 8 6 4 2

ISBN: 0-00-718905-2

The Contender Entertainment Group
48 Margaret Street London W1W 8SE
www.tractortom.com
Tractor Tom © Contender Ltd 2002
A CIP catalogue record for this title is available from the British Library.

TRACTOR TOM AND FRIENDS
STORY AND ACTIVITY BOOK

HarperCollins *Children's Books*

CONTENTS

MEET THE GANG!

TRACTOR TOM
Brave Tractor Tom always saves the day! What would we do without him?

FARMER FI
Kind and caring, she works hard on Springhill Farm all year long and looks after everyone who lives there.

FARMHAND MATT
Helps Fi out with all the jobs she has to do and is full of great ideas – some of which turn out to be not so great!

BUZZ
Young, zippy and fun – Buzz the quad bike is also full of mischief and sometimes quite naughty!

REV
A big, strong, shiny purple pick-up truck. Rev's engine has a very loud roar!

MO
Gentle and friendly, Mo the cow gives Fi her milk every morning.

RIFF
Sensible Riff is a very good sheep dog. She's always tidying up!

PURDEY
Sleepy farm cat Purdey's favourite things are lapping up cream and then dozing off in a comfortable spot.

WACK AND BACH
The Springhill Farm ducks – they are a little crazy!

WHEEZY
He might be a little older than the rest but at harvest time Wheezy the combine is hard at work on the farm.

THE SHEEP
Who knows what these naughty, mischievous sheep will do next? They're always up to something.

SNICKER
Winnie's naughty young foal who just loves causing trouble with his best friend Buzz.

WINNIE
A beautiful horse who can sometimes be a little bit forgetful.

TREASURE TRAIL

Everybody at Springhill Farm was very excited. That night, Fi was having a bonfire party. Tom had one little job to do – take an old cupboard and put it on the bonfire.

Fi thought she had better check there was nothing inside it first.

When she came to the last drawer, Fi found some old photos. "This is my grandad. He was a soldier, you know!" said Fi, pointing to one of the photos.

"Just look at all his medals! He must have been really brave!" she said proudly.

Matt was getting ready to spend the morning on his new hobby. "It's a metal detector, Rev," he explained, as he switched on the machine. "You use it to look for metal things." "Bonggg!" went the machine, as it clanked onto Rev's bonnet!

"Oops, sorry, Rev!" said Matt. "I must have had it turned up too high."

Tom and Fi took the old cupboard to put it on the bonfire.
But when Tom broke it up, Fi noticed something.
"Hang on – what's that?" wondered Fi.
It was a mysterious box.

"It's locked and I can't open it," she said.
"I'll try again later when I have time."

Later, when Fi had gone to have lunch, Buzz, Wheezy and Tom tried to open the box for her. They tried everything but it just wouldn't open.

They did find something on the bottom of it though – a set of initials and a keyhole!

Matt thought he had found some treasure with the metal detector. But it wasn't gold coins or a diamond ring. It was an old bath! Rev couldn't help laughing, then Tom joined in, and then the sheep started! Baa ha ha ha ha!
"Well, I'm off," sulked Matt.

"And you can do what you like with that silly, rotten, smelly old bath!" So off the sheep went to play with the bath.

Back at the barn, Wheezy and Buzz were showing Fi
what they had found.
"These are my grandad's initials!" cried Fi. "The box
must have belonged to him! And look, there's a keyhole!"
Fi shook the box. They could hear something clinking inside!

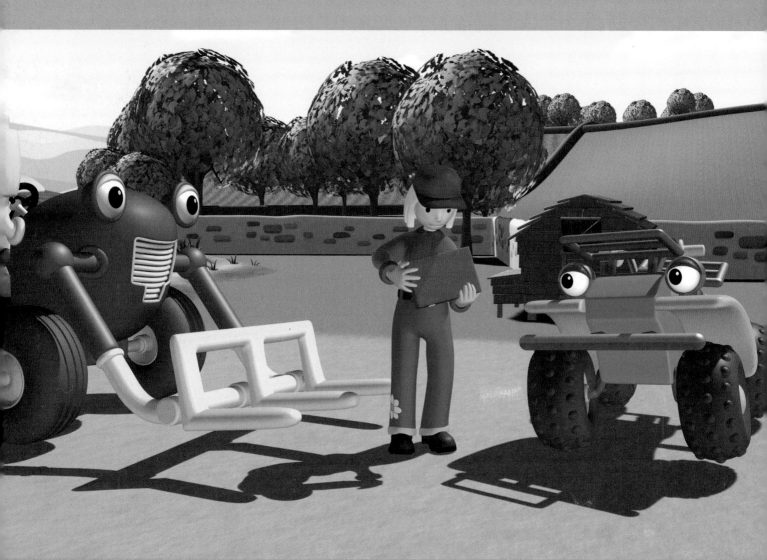

"Oh, if only we knew where the key was!" she said.
Then Tom had an idea...

Tom thought the key might be somewhere in the broken bits
of old cupboard on the bonfire.

But it was like looking for a needle in a haystack.
Poor Tom didn't find anything.

Later that day, Matt was surprised to see the rusty old bath moving.
"Help, I'm being chased by an old tin bath. Tom, save me!" shouted Matt, tripping over Tom! But when Tom lifted the upside down bath it was only a SHEEP underneath!

"Hey! What's all the noise about? I thought this was supposed to be a bonfire party!" said Fi.

The fireworks at the bonfire party were fantastic but Tom was rather sad. He was sure that the key to the mysterious box was now lost forever somewhere in the bonfire. Or was it?

Tom had another idea! He bobbed up and down with excitement. But it would have to wait until the next day.

The next morning, Tom went back to the ashes of the bonfire with Matt and the metal detector.
"You want me to look for treasure HERE, Tom?" asked Matt.
Just then, the metal detector began to beep loudly.

"Hang on, what's this?" said Matt, hooking out a key!
Fi put the key into the box's lock and turned it.

When they have finished all the jobs for the day, Farmer Fi says "Well done, Tom!"

DRAW A PICTURE

Look, it's Winnie and Snicker!

Now copy the picture
into the grid below!

MATCH THE PAIRS

Can you help Riff to find all the pairs?
Draw lines between the things that match.
Who is left over?

A SURPRISE FOR FI

It was a very special day at Springhill Farm – Farmer Fi's birthday!

"Happy birthday!" said Matt. "When does the party start?"

"Not until I find Riff," worried Fi. "She's disappeared!"

Farmer Fi's sheepdog, Riff, had gone missing. Tractor Tom wanted to help find her, so he and Farmer Fi went off to search. When they had gone, Matt started to make plans...

"Fi hasn't got time to arrange a birthday party, so we'll have to do it for her. Right, first job is to make a cake. You all know what to do!"

Buzz brought flour. There were eggs from the hens.
Mo carried a pail of milk. At last, Matt put the cake into the oven in Fi's kitchen.

Tractor Tom and Farmer Fi were busy searching for Riff.
"Baa-ba-ba-ba-ba," sang the sheep, to the tune of 'Happy birthday to you'.
"Thank you," said Fi, "but I'm not having a birthday until I find Riff. Have any of you seen her?"

"Baaa!"
"No? Oh, dear. Come on, Tom. We'll have to search the whole farm," said Fi.

Matt, Mo, Snicker, Wack and Bach decorated the barn for the party.
"Now what else do we need?" wondered Matt.

"No, Wheezy, I don't think Fi wants a gallon of engine oil with her tea. But she will want food. What am I going to do? I know – pizza!"

Matt rushed out of the barn to find Rev.

"Rev, I need you to go into Beckton and get take-away pizza for us all. And remember, no olives for Fi. And extra cheese for the sheep. Quick as you can," called Matt.

It didn't take Rev long to bring back the pizzas from Beckton. Then disaster struck! A branch had fallen from a tree and blocked the road.

Rev drove straight into it and the pizza flew up into the air! It landed on his windscreen and slid down messily. Oh, dear!

Back at the farm, Matt was wondering where Rev had got to.
"Can you go and find him, Buzz?" he asked.
Buzz sped off, and soon found Rev stuck behind the fallen
branch.

He could see that it was a real emergency... the pizzas were
getting cold! It was a job for Tractor Tom!

Buzz and Rev couldn't move the tree trunk, but it was no trouble for Tom.

On the way back, Tom suddenly thought of one place that Fi hadn't looked for Riff.

Back at Springhill Farm, Fi was feeling very sad.
"This has been the worst birthday I've ever had," she said.
"Maybe a party would cheer you up..." suggested Matt.
"No, all I want to do is find Riff," explained Fi.

Just then, Tom appeared behind them and swept
Fi up onto his forks. Tom rushed up the hill to the one place
where they hadn't looked for Riff... Matt's caravan!

When Fi looked inside Matt's caravan she got a very special surprise.
"That's where Riff was! She was having puppies!" cried Fi.
"Oh, Riff. They're beautiful!"
"And now we can start your birthday," said Matt happily.

"And it'll be extra special because it's the puppies' birthday too!" agreed Farmer Fi.

"Happy birthday, Fi!" said everyone. There were lots of presents...From Mo, a pair of gloves to keep Fi's hands warm when she was milking.
The 'Combine Harvester Book of Corny Jokes' from Wheezy...
A quad bike CD player from Buzz. A big feather duster from

Wack and Bach and the hens – made with their own feathers.
A hub cap from Rev. A new saddle from Snicker and Winnie.
A pot of cream from Purdey. A new shirt from Matt.

"Thank you, everyone. But I think Tom brought me the best present of all. He found Riff and her puppies!"
"What would we do without him?" laughed Matt.

"What would I do without you all?" smiled Fi.
And everyone cheered happily.

TOM'S
PICTURE
PUZZLE

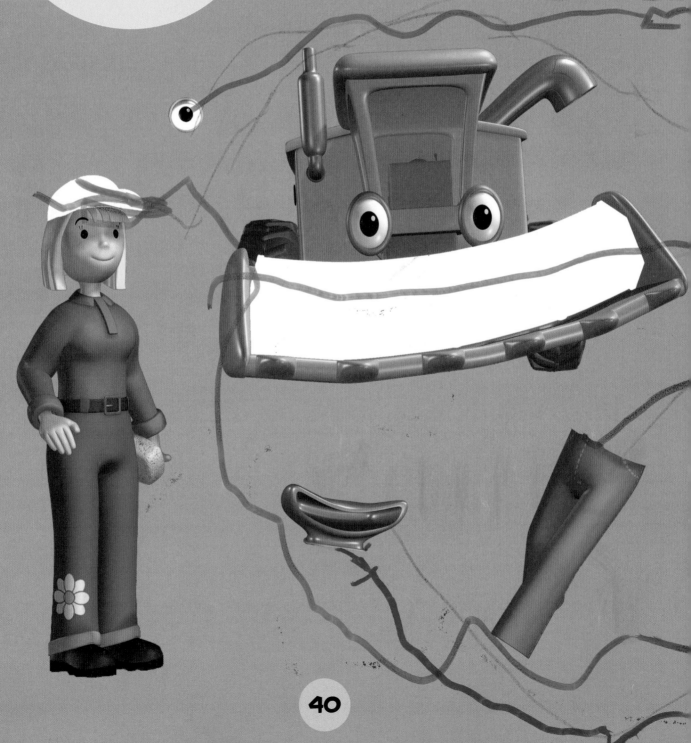

Oh, dear! Each of these
pictures has a little bit missing.
Can you point to the
missing piece?

COLOUR REV AND MATT

Matt and Rev are very busy today!
Colour the picture and make a noise like Rev's
powerful engine. Brrrrrrrm, Brrrrrrrm!

"Time for an oil change," says Matt. Can you find the tool box? Now colour the rest of the picture!

LOTS OF THINGS TO FIND

There's lots to see in this picture.
Can you spot all the things in this list?
Tick the boxes as you go – it's fun.

BAA BAA TOM SHEEP

It was lambing time at Springhill Farm. Tom and Fi had come to feed the sheep. But the sheep were nowhere to be found. "Where have they gone?" asked Fi.

Someone had left the gate open. Riff and Fi went to find out where the sheep were.

Matt was busy loading up Rev and Buzz with honey and flour. Suddenly, his mobile phone rang. It was Fi asking him to look for the sheep.

When Matt left, Rev and Buzz, who were feeling naughty, decided to have a race!
Ready, steady, go!

They raced out of the farm. Tom was waiting for Fi beside the bridge. As Buzz flew over the bridge the honey jars fell off his carrier and smashed all over Tom!

Then, as Rev raced over the bridge, the bag of flour bounced out of his carrier and that went all over Tom too!
Now Tom was white all over!

Tom was still covered in flour when a little lamb came by.
"Ma-ma!" said the lamb.
Just then, Fi and Riff returned.

Fi spotted the lamb and decided to take her back to the farm to
get her some milk. But the little lamb wouldn't drink.
She kept trying to go back to Tom.

Then Matt and Fi had a brilliant idea. They tied a bottle of milk to the front of Tom! Soon the lamb was happily drinking the milk. "She thinks that Tom is her mummy," said Fi. "But we need to find her real mother."

Matt offered to help. "I'll do that," he said. "I'm good with sheep."

Wherever Tom went that day the little lamb was sure to go. She even tried to help Tom plough the field by pulling a stick in her mouth. No matter how hard Matt tried he couldn't get the little lamb to stay in the field with the other sheep.

Matt even tried to show the lamb how to act like a sheep. "You are a lamb, not a tractor," he said. "You eat grass, you do little lamby jumps in the air, and you drink water from the river," he explained, as he walked by the water's edge.

Suddenly, there was a big splash! Matt had fallen into the river!

"Hey, who's been chucking rubbish in here?" he shouted, pulling a pram out of the water.

The little lamb ran all the way back to Tom.
Fi thought it would help the little lamb to find her mummy if Tom
stayed with her, and the other sheep, in the field.
Tom wasn't very happy with this idea. He had lots of work to do
on the farm.

"I think you make a wonderful mummy," said Matt, smiling.

Meanwhile, naughty Buzz and Rev decided to have another race. They flew out of the farmyard and through the field.

They went so fast they scared the little lamb, who fell into the river! Tom rushed to save her.

Tom bravely drove further into the river to stop the little lamb from being swept away. The water in the river washed off all the honey and flour. Tom was no longer white.
Back in the field the lamb looked at Tom, but now she didn't think he was her mummy.

"Ma-ma!" she called. And ran over to the other sheep.

"I've got an idea," said Matt. And he went to get the pram he had found in the river.
He put one of the sheep inside the pram and the little lamb ran up to it calling, "Ma-ma!"

"Well done, Matt," said Fi. "The lamb thought that Tom was her mum when he looked like a sheep and now this sheep looks a bit like Tractor Tom!"

Back at the farmyard Fi and Matt cleaned and polished Tom.
"I'm glad we got that lamb sorted out," said Matt. "You know
how sheep can be once they get an idea into their heads."
"Oh, no! Look!" shouted Fi.

All the sheep had pram wheels and were racing down the hill.
"They all want to be tractor-sheep!" laughed Fi!

COLOUR TOM AND FRIENDS

Tom and all his friends live at Springhill Farm. Now you can colour them all in this great big picture!

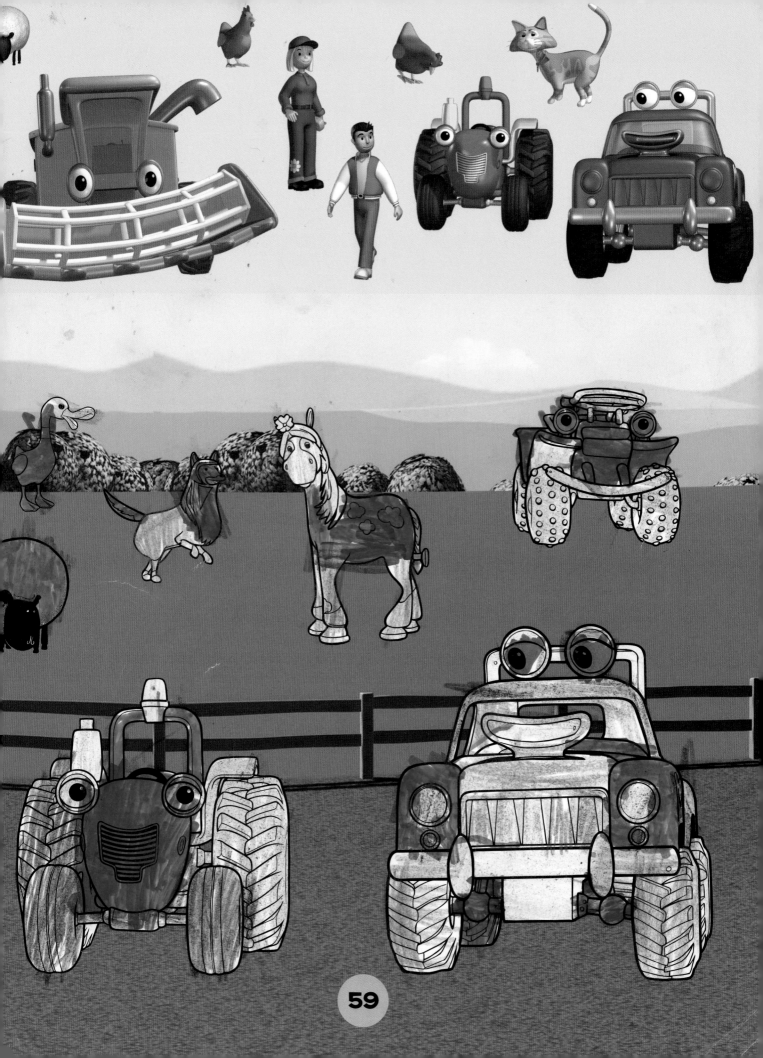

SHADOW GAME

Can you help Tractor Tom
to match up all these animals
with their shadows?

COUNT TO 10
WITH TRACTOR TOM

How many can you see?

1 one handy tool box
2 two noisy ducks
3 three naughty hens
4 four tall trees
5 five smiley scarecrows

6 six fun footballs
7 seven silly sheep
8 eight slippery fish
9 nine fresh eggs
10 ten delicious apples

A JOB FOR BUZZ

It was a busy day at Springhill Farm. Tom and Fi had lots of jobs to do. Buzz was very keen to help, but every time he did he got in the way. When he tried to stop Mo eating the hay, he almost crashed into Tom!

"Buzz!" cried Fi. "This work is too difficult for you.
Leave it to Tom."

That night, Buzz was very cross that he hadn't been allowed to work at all. Tom got all the best jobs on the farm.

Buzz didn't like this so he came up with a very naughty plan...

The next day Farmer Fi was up bright and early to get Tom, "Come on, Tom. It's going to be another busy day," she called. But Tom's engine wouldn't start. Fi had a lot of work to do. What was she going to do without Tom?

Buzz rushed up. "Do you think you can do Tom's jobs for today?" Fi asked.

But Buzz couldn't pull the trailer because it was too heavy. He couldn't move the sheep because they played tricks on him. And when he tried to move the bales of hay he nearly had an accident!

"It's no use, Buzz, you just aren't strong enough," said Fi.

Matt was trying to work out what was wrong with Tom.
He asked Rev to pull Tom to the top of Beckton Hill so they could
bump start him. Tom was worried.

"Hey, don't worry," laughed Matt. "It is a great idea and it's
bound to get you working again."

When they got to the top of Beckton Hill Rev thought he would give Tom a helping hand.
Suddenly, Tom started to roll down the hill!
Faster and faster he went.

Over the bridge and into the farm, where he crashed into the hen house!

Back at the field Fi could hear one of the hens calling and went to look.

"Oh, no!" she cried. It was stuck in some brambles.

Fi tried to help the hen, but she got caught in the brambles too.

Buzz tried to free Fi, but he couldn't do it.

"It's no good," she said. "Go and get Tom!"

So Buzz rushed off to the barn to get Tom.
"What's wrong?" asked Matt "Has something happened to Fi?
Tom can't help, he's still broken."

Buzz raced towards Matt and lifted him off his feet, then carried
him to the hen house.

"What are you doing?" shouted Matt. "Is there something in the hen house?" Matt looked inside the hen house and found a piece of Tom's engine.

"How did this get here?" he asked. Buzz looked guilty. "Never mind, at least we can fix Tom now," said Matt.

Matt and Buzz fixed Tom, then Tom went to rescue Fi.

"Thanks for mending Tom, Matt," said Fi.

"That's ok," replied Matt. "I had some help from Buzz, but I think he might have had something to do with Tom breaking down in the first place."

"Bu-zz!" said Buzz, apologising.

Tom and Buzz were soon very busy doing a whole days work. "Well done," said Fi. "What would we do without you, Tom?"

As Tom went off to the barn Buzz tried to follow him. "Where are you going, Buzz?" called Fi. "I have got one more really important job especially for you!"

Fi knew Buzz had only been naughty because he wanted to feel as important as Tractor Tom, so she gave him a very special job to do.

"Stopping the sheep from causing trouble is one job that he's just right for," smiled Fi.

OLOUR FI, BU ..., WINNIE AND SNICKER

Fi and Buzz are on their
way to the stables to check on
Winnie and Snicker!

"There you are!" says Fi.
Snicker is very happy to see
his friend Buzz.
Can you add some
colour to this picture?

ANIMAL SOUNDS

NEIGH

MOOO

CLUCK

Point to the animals and
make their sounds – can you match
all the words and pictures?

QUACK

MEOW

WOOF

BAAAA

A BUSY DAY ON SPRINGHILL FARM

MORNING

In the morning, Tractor Tom collects Fi from the farmhouse. Fi's first jobs are to milk Mo and collect the eggs while Tractor Tom stacks barrels in the barn.

LUNCHTIME

It's feeding time for the animals there's hay for the horses, seed for the hens and some tasty cat food for Purdey the cat.

EVENING

Riff rounds up the sheep in the field while Tractor Tom and Fi tidy up the yard ready for another busy day tomorrow!

ANSWERS

There's lots to see in this picture. Can you spot all the things in this list? Tick the boxes as you go – it's fun.

SHADOW GAME

60

MATCH THE PAIRS

Can you help Riff to find all pairs? Who is left over?

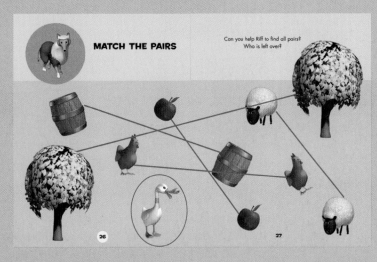

26   27

ANIMAL SOUNDS

Point to the animals and make their sounds – can you match all the words and pictures?

NEIGH   QUACK

MEOW

WOOF

BAAAA

MOOO   CLUCK

78   79

TOM'S PICTURE PUZZLE

Oh, dear! Each of these pictures has a little bit missing. Can you point to the missing piece?

40   41

TRACTOR TOM'S SPORTS DAY

It was a very special day on Springhill Farm. The postman had brought a surprise parcel for Tractor Tom. Fi went outside to open it.

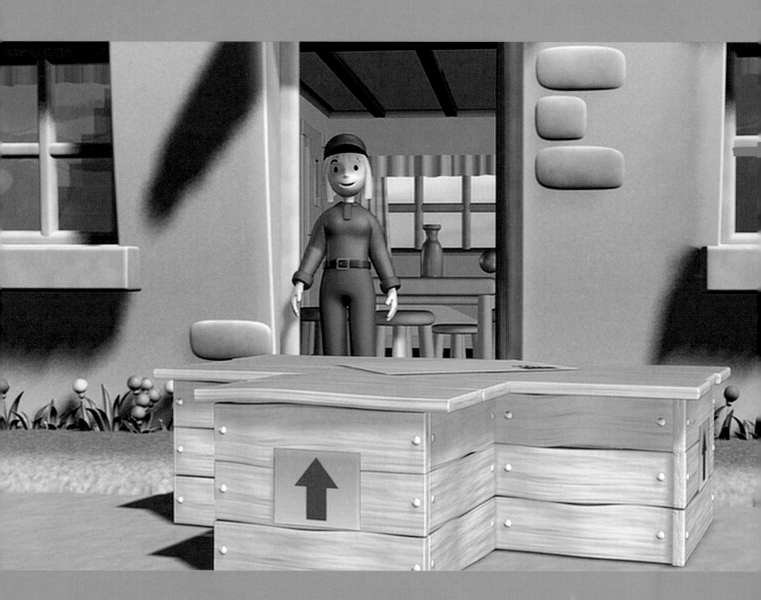

"It's a new mower to help Tom cut the grass!" said Fi. Tractor Tom was very excited. He couldn't wait to get the new mower attached and try it out for the very first time!

It was a special day for Matt too. He was getting ready for the sports day in Beckton. Matt really wanted to win his race so he was doing lots of exercises to make sure he was really fit.

"Phew!" he gasped as he finished a sit-up and leapt to his feet to go for a run around the farm.

In the field, Tom was busy making wide stripes of neatly cut grass with the new mower. Tom loved his new mower. It was really fast.

"Well done, Tom!" said Fi. "We'll cut the grass in this field in no time!"

Just then, Matt jogged past Tom and Fi's field.
"Hello, Matt!" called Fi, "What are you doing?"
"I'm doing some last minute practise for the Beckton Sports Day," cried Matt.

"I want to be ready to beat everyone in my race – and it's nearly time to go!"

Matt was just about to leave with Rev for the Beckton Sports Day when his mobile phone rang.
"Oh, no!" Matt told Rev, "The ground in Beckton is flooded – they can't have a sports day after all!"

Matt was very disappointed. He went to tell Fi and Tom.

Matt told Fi and Tom all about the flood. Tom knew just what to do to cheer him up! "Tom-tom, tom-tom!" he told Fi. "Tom thinks we should have our own sports day right here in our newly mown field!" said Fi.

"What a great idea!"

Everyone got ready for the first race. Wheezy, Purdey and Winnie waited nervously for the start.
"Ready...steady...go!" shouted Fi.
Wheezy rumbled into life and headed rather slowly towards the finishing line.

But Winnie began eating the grass and when they looked, Purdey had fallen asleep, so Wheezy won easily!
"Congratulations, Wheezy!" everyone cried.

Next it was time for the egg and spoon race!
"Come on, Fi, it's your turn now," said Matt.
"On your marks…get set…go!" he shouted. They were off!
Fi, Riff and Snicker ran as fast as they could…oops!

Riff dropped her egg and was out of the race!
Snicker galloped even harder and just beat Fi to the finish line.
Well done, Snicker!

The last race of the day was the six-legged race for the sheep! "Ready…steady…go!" shouted Fi for the last time.

The sheep soon tumbled over each other and ended up riding on each other's backs. They got the loudest cheer of the day as they finished…all at the same time!

Fi and Matt shared a special sports day cup – a nice cup of tea!
"Thank you for organising the best sports day ever, Fi,"
said Matt.

"Don't thank me," smiled Fi, "Thank Tom. He cut the grass so
quickly, we had somewhere to hold our own sports day."
"Tom – what would we do without you?" cheered Matt.

0-00-7189044 £5.99

OLLECT THEM ALL!

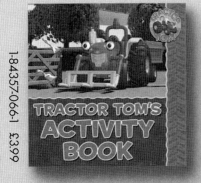

1-84357-066-1 £3.99

TRACTOR TOM'S ACTIVITY BOOK

1-84357-064-5 £3.99

TRACTOR TOM AND THE MOBILE PHONE

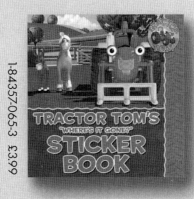

1-84357-065-3 £3.99

TRACTOR TOM'S "WHERE'S IT GONE?" STICKER BOOK

O WITHOUT HIM?

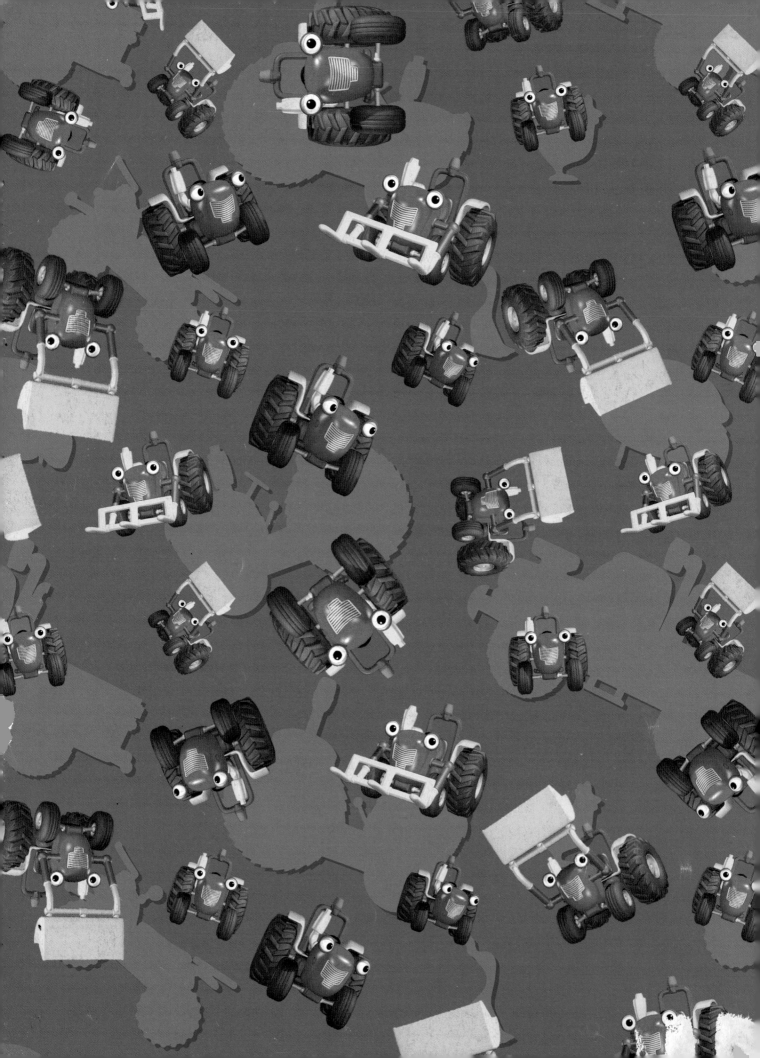